Tale of the L

MW01017166

by

Kyra Dawson

Illustrations by Candice McMullan

Editor Rosie Reay

The Persimmon Tales - Book 1

For a complete glossary of terms and places used in this novel,
as well as full character persona descriptions,
please visit www.persimmontales.com.

Kyra Dawson

Tale of the Lost Swan Egg

by

Kyra Dawson

Illustrations by Candice McMullan

Editor Rosie Reay

Children's fiction. Also children's travel and educational series.

First published Dec 2010 by Foden Press
www.fodenpress.com

ISBN 978-0-9710157-2-2

In praise of *Tale of the Lost Swan Egg.*

A very good descriptive work. Makes you feel like you are really there and are involved in the the story. Also the illustrations are just wonderful and all of my five children really enjoyed listening to the story. They asked a lot of questions about what is going to happen next.

Claire Lynas, UK Mother of Five.

This is a most delightful, informative, and well put together children's book. It is refreshing to read a fictional story that subtly includes so many real facts for children to easily learn from. Kyra has truly brought 3-D to children's literature! Great depth of character, use of descriptive words and, inclusion of factual information. The story and characters come alive and draw you right into the plot. Both of my boys took delight in hearing and learning from this wonderful story.

Vicki J., Canada, Mother of two busy boys.

Remember the books your parents read to you when you were sick to make you feel better? They were heart-warming and endearing but written so long ago you had to stop your parents every few minutes to ask, "What's that?". The Tale of the Lost Swan Egg will be sure to become one of your child's favorite, "Read me a story," books, but written in today's miraculous world they will be sure to understand. It's a great read for all.

Sean H., Florida, USA

The stories behind the characters lives are written so well, you get to know who they are and what they are about. Each character is descriptively different. Surely favourites will be chosen while the tale unfolds, for a lasting adventure which is definitely not your typical run of the mill kids book with weak plots, boring climaxes, and flat endings.

The "Tale of the Lost Swan Egg" will leave children smiling and holding their breath, and laughing along the way. This unforgettable book will possibly make mommies tear up, and sear the imaginations and dreams of all through the wonderful world of Persimmon.

H. Ulrich, Canada, A very impressed Mom.

A delightful, and charming read. It has been some time since I've read a children's story that has captivated me as this one has. A rising star in children's literature, and definitely one to watch. I look forward to more from this author.

V. Annur. Brooklyn, NY

This book is dedicated to Heather.

The love of my life, my reason for everything.

Kyra Dawson

A Note from Persimmon

Stanley Park isn't like a regular park at all. It is more like a large forest on a peninusula connected to the city of Vancouver in British Columbia. It is a much loved and popular green space that even has two lakes! Beaver Lake is one of them, but it is Lost Lagoon that is my personal favorite. Stanley Park is a world quite different from the rush of the city right next door.

Salmonberries grow on wooden stemmed thickets, and wildflowers sprinkle the grass with color. Ferns and all kinds of mosses grow everywhere, and the trees are huge, huge, huge! If you stand very still, you can feel the green things breathing and living all around you. You may even feel a hushed magic surrounding you as you stand safe beneath the sleepy trees, in the sun dappled secrets of the forest park.

Every day in any season, you can find people enjoying the beauty and peacefulness of Stanley Park. Every day you can see them laughing and playing or walking their dogs. It's fun to walk across the bridges and play in the playgrounds before exploring the trails while you discover the mysteries of nature.

There are beaches where kids can build sand castles, find shells and seaweed. The ocean waves can wash right over your feet and tickle your toes as you watch the large ships and boats sitting in English Bay. The Sea Wall is a pathway perfect for biking and goes right around the whole park for 10 km. That would be a very long walk, but can you imagine how much fun riding your bike on this path would be?

The very best part of Stanley Park is the animals that live there. There are ducks and eagles and herons and swans. Raccoons run around and squirrels climb the trees. Otters swim in Lost Lagoon and Pacific Harbor seals splash in the sea. If you're very lucky, you may even catch a glimpse of orcas, or dolphins, or even whales! There are bugs and frogs, even butterflies. There are skunks and minks and muskrats, too.

Stanley Park is alive with wildlife. It's a fun place to live. It's my home. My name is Persimmon. I am a Snowshoe Hare, and a Snowshoe Hare in Stanley Park is a rare sight indeed!

Chapter One

Persimmon Hare stepped out of his house onto the back porch. He stood for a moment, looking at the thick cover of leaves of the trees and the shrubs that surrounded his cozy little house. Last night from his bedroom window, Persimmon had seen little lights flitting like fireflies. Only they hadn't been fireflies, of that he was sure. These little fluttering and zooming lights had been like the colors of the rainbow, glowing like the flashing lights on a Christmas tree. This morning there seemed to be no sign of them.

Persimmon typed a quick reminder into his Blackberry. Tonight at 10 o'clock he would be ready. He would wait, hidden in his neighbor's dense thicket, his fancy camera ready to take pictures of those strange lights. Perhaps he would even post the pictures in the *Stanley Park Tattler* and write a little article to go with it. He could see the title of his article now in big bold letters splashed across the front page, "Mystery Lights Captured on Film in Stanley Park!" How exciting! He loved a good mystery. Perhaps he could even solve it.

Content and happy with his plans for the evening, Persimmon stretched and yawned. It was early yet, and his parents Mr. and Mrs. Cottontail were still in bed fast asleep. The sun had barely begun to peek its golden head over the tops of the giant trees in Stanley Park. Not even the early birds were up and singing yet. It was Persimmon's favorite time of day, when everything was still and the air was damp and cool. He took a deep breath of the chilly air and wiggled his ears, tail and toes.

Persimmon Hare was unlike any other hare you will ever meet. He was a Snowshoe Hare, the only one in all of Stanley Park. His coat was white all year round, except for the black tips of his ears and the black smudging around his whiskers. This was a typical Snowshoe trait; what wasn't typical was that Persimmon had never turned cinnamon brown. Not ever, not one bit, not even during the hottest part of summer. He was a hare that definitely stood out in a crowd; especially since Vancouver isn't known to be a place where it snows a lot.

His eyes were the deep purple hue of the heather flower, and his nose was Persimmon red, which was why he was named Persimmon. He had huge feet, the hugest feet a hare could have. The bunnies who lived in Stanley Park teased him good naturedly about the size of his feet, but Persimmon didn't mind. Someday he would take a trip to Alaska and Greenland and hop upon the snow. And that was something those Easter bunnies would not be able to do. And of course he sported the little white cotton tail, which he did mind; but everyone else thought it was the cutest thing because it was so, well, cute and cottony.

He liked to wear his lucky, dark blue, V-neck sweater vest. Underneath he wore a white button down shirt with the sleeves rolled up and the collar loosened. But he fancied it up with a yellow tie that had thin blue stripes. In the back of this tie there was a nifty little pocket for his Blackberry.

Persimmon loved his Blackberry and wouldn't trade it for anything. He always had his Blackberry with him. He liked to use the phone for email as well, and sometimes even for the occasional text. Texting wasn't his favorite thing to do, but it came in handy when you were in a rush to send and receive information. He also loved the built in camera because one never knew when going about their day that one would need to take a picture.

Yes, a Snowshoe Hare in Stanley Park is an unusual sight to be sure, but being unusual is what Persimmon did best. He dreamed of deep sea diving, and swimming with the orcas, and maybe even finding sunken treasure. He wanted to travel the world, writing and taking pictures, and surfing every ocean that one could surf in the world. These were fantastic dreams, and Persimmon dreamed them every day.

Persimmon lived with his mother and father, Mr. and Mrs. Cottontail, who happen to be bunnies and not hares, but that is another story. They lived in the hollow of a towering, hollow, old growth spruce tree that was full of green needled branches. The great tree was surrounded by hemlocks and three types of fern. There were also red huckleberry bushes and salmonberry thickets that became heavily laden with ripe and juicy berries in the fall.

Being that the tree was old and very large meant it was very spacious inside. There were two floors above ground and two below. The two floors below were used for food storage and his dad's old fashioned photo lab. On the main floor was the kitchen, the dining room and the living room. Upstairs in the front was his mom and dad's room and the bathroom.

Persimmon's room was at the back. He had two windows in his room, one big and one small. The big one was a casement window that opened inward and sat over a window seat. From here Persimmon could look out over the back yard. The second window was little and round on the adjacent wall, on the east side of the tree house. From this window, Persimmon would look out through the brambles both day and night, watching the swans on Lost Lagoon and other goings on in his woodland neighborhood.

Persimmon checked his Blackberry. No calls. No new messages. Wow. It was a quiet morning. He looked at the barn shaped shed at the end of his backyard. Maybe he would finish painting his surfboard before heading over to Lost Lagoon to visit the swans and their little egg. He started to head over to the shed when suddenly there was a flitting and hum in his right ear.

"Good morning, Persimmon!" squeaked a teeny tiny little voice. Persimmon turned his head to the right, ready to greet his visitor. There was nobody there.

"Over here, Persimmon," said that cheery little voice again. This time the humming buzz was at his left ear. Persimmon turned his head quick as a wink.

"Good morning, Pippin!" Persimmon greeted the hummingbird. "How is your wife Mairi? And the new chicks?"

"Fine and feathered!" answered Pippin, darting over to the porch where the pretty pink hummingbird feeder hung. He hovered close to the feeder, sipping the sweet sugar water Persimmon filled it with every other day. "She is getting them ready for breakfast as we speak!" Pippin's little wings zoomed furiously fast, creating that wonderful humming sound that Persimmon loved so much.

"Excellent!" Persimmon exclaimed. He couldn't wait to see the two little chicks. He had promised Mairi that he'd take a series of pictures over the next two weeks. He had already taken a bunch of pictures of the chicks when they were just two wee white eggs tucked into a nest of spider silk, lichens and plant down. Now that they were hatched, Persimmon couldn't wait to see them.

"Well, Pippin, I've got to get going to the lagoon. How's about a quick picture? I have pictures of everyone except for you," Persimmon said, trying to persuade the camera shy hummingbird to pose for a picture.

"Welllll, I don't know…" Pippin stammered, nervously darting from left to right as if looking for an escape route. He had forgotten all about sipping the sugar water from his feeder.

"Don't worry. Just act natural. Pretend I'm not even here and you are just eating your breakfast as usual."

"Ah, like this?" Pippin squeaked, his long beak tapping against the feeder spout in his agitation. His left eye rolled back at

Persimmon, trying to keep the hare in his sight. His little body began to quiver and his wings flapped even faster when Persimmon raised the Blackberry's camera.

"Not quite, don't look at me. Think about bugs and nectar," Persimmon said soothingly.

"Right, bugs and nectar," Pippin repeated, his words muffled because he was trying not to open his beak. "Should I smile?"

"If you like," Persimmon said agreeably. "Ready?"

"Bugs and nectar. Cheese!" exclaimed Pippin, and Persimmon snapped the picture.

"Let's see it!" Pippin nearly shouted, and buzzed over in a rush and hovered over Persimmon's Blackberry nervously.

When the digital picture appeared, it showed a grimacing hummingbird with his eyes wide open in alarm.

"Er, well, it does take some practice," Persimmon offered hesitantly.

"Oh well," Pippin shrugged, grimacing again, "that is why Mairi won't let me in any of the family pictures. You can't be good at everything! Besides, I'm better in person."

"Maybe you could practice in front of a mirror first," Persimmon suggested.

"What are you two on about so early in the morning?" a voice asked out of the blue, startling Persimmon and Pippin so much that they jumped.

It was Gilly, Persimmon's next door neighbor. Gilly was a large white and butterscotch guinea pig. "Call me Gilly," he always said whenever introducing himself, "like the gills of a fish! Gilly, that's me!"

Gilly lived in a spacious little burrow on the other side of the salmonberry thicket, and every day on his way to Lost Lagoon, Persimmon passed by Gilly's place. The entrance to Gilly's little house was little more than a little hole with a little round door. It was just large enough for him to squeeze his well rounded guinea pig body through. On the nicely swept doorstep there was a little welcome mat, and a pot of marigolds on either side of his door. Even still, if one didn't know where to find the doorway, it could easily be missed.

Gilly liked to wear the most outrageous outfits. He had dinosaur costumes, a yellow ducky costume, and a penguin costume. He had four kinds of bear costumes, a polar bear, a panda bear, a grizzly bear and the whimsical Spirit bear. He told the most wonderful stories of a time before he lived next door to Persimmon in the woods of Stanley Park. These stories always started with once upon a time and were filled with palaces and humans, technology and noise.

Now Gilly was a very friendly type. But he could be cranky when his salmonberry thicket became shabby or unkempt, or the birds ate all of the berries. At those times you would hear him muttering to himself about lodging a complaint with the president of The Bird Network, although he never did.

Almost every day Gilly could be found tending his little garden that was filled with carrots, lettuces, parsley, cilantro, cherry to-matoes, spinach, broccoli and cucumbers. He also grew straw-berries and cultivated a nice wild patch of dandelion greens. He was always nibbling. From sunup to sundown it seemed his little jaws were always moving at a frenzied pace.

Gilly had popped his head up from tending his garden. As usu-al, he was chewing something rapidly and had a bag of carrot seeds in his hands. He was wearing his blue dinosaur suit with the yellow triangular spikes that went down his back to the tail. Persimmon was certain it was the Stegosaurus suit.

"What are you two whispering about over there so early in the morn? The fog is still about and the sun is barely up!" This Gilly said with a lisp while looking at Persimmon and Pippin suspiciously, chewing all the while. He seemed to have forgot-ten all about the carrot seeds he was holding.

"Well, I'm off to see what is keeping Mairi and the chicks," Pippin said sheepishly, embarrassed by the whole picture taking fiasco. He wondered how long Gilly had been watching them. And without another word, Pippin zoomed off home.

"Oh, good morning, Gilly," Persimmon answered politely, his heather hued eyes sparkling and his red nose twitching. He was trying very hard not to laugh. He walked towards Gilly, stopping at the salmonberry thicket and peering over the greenery that separated Gilly's home from Persimmon's own. "I'm off to see the swans and their egg. Maybe it hatched during the night. Maybe there is a cygnet there now!" Persimmon was ever so pleased that he knew baby swans were called cygnets.

"Well, I'm sure Curly Squirrelly would be shouting from the treetops before even the crows knew what was up if there was any news to be had, and as of yet all is quiet."

Gilly's head disappeared momentarily and reappeared just as suddenly, and Persimmon covered his mouth with a paw to hide his grin. He cleared his throat to stifle his laughing. Dandelion greens were sticking out every which way from the guinea pig's mouth. Despite Persimmon's best efforts, a laugh slipped out. The way Gilly's cheeks moved as he chewed with quick, nibbly bites was priceless. Persimmon coughed, trying once again to disguise his laughter, but if Gilly noticed, he didn't say anything.

"I think you will find an egg in the nest yet, my boy. Be sure to bring me news of the Big Event when it happens. Unfortunately and as you know, I may be unable to attend," Gilly requested as the dandelion greens disappeared with a flash of teeth.

It was a sure fact of the park that Gilly was a known hermit who never left the boundaries of his domain hardly ever if at all. He had once said that living in the confines of a cage had removed all taste of adventure from his mind, and he much preferred the safety of his burrow.

"I will, I promise!" Persimmon said with a grin, waving his little paw hastily and turning away, dashing toward Lost Lagoon.

As Gilly watched Persimmon's little cotton tail disappearing across the trail, he scratched his head, popping dandelion greens into his mouth. "I wonder where he is going in such a hurry?" Gilly asked aloud and to no one in particular..

***

While making his way to Lost Lagoon, a splash of black color among the green caught Persimmon's eye. He decided to stop by the little duck pond where Curly Squirrelly was standing in the tall grasses surrounding the edges of the pool. As usual,

Curly was tugging on his ears as if in distress, and Persimmon wondered how the squirrel managed to ever hear anything.

"Psst! Curly!" Persimmon whispered right next to the squirrel's ear. He chuckled when the squirrel jumped into the air nearly landing in the pond, squeaking in surprise.

"Oh my gosh, Persimmon! Shame on you!" the little black squirrel chattered in his high pitched voice.

Persimmon patted the squirrel on his shoulder. "I'm sorry, Curly, I couldn't help it! And you were tugging at your ears again. What if I had been a fox?" At this, Curly Squirrelly began tugging his poor ears once again.

"There are no foxes in Stanley Park, Persimmon," Curly declared, yet he still tugged worriedly at his ears. "Coyotes on the other hand… Yikes!" and Curly's entire body shuddered.

"Don't worry, Curly. I haven't seen a coyote in months," Persimmon soothed the squirrel. He reached into the pocket of his shirt beneath his sweater vest and produced a sunflower seed and handed it to Curly. The seed distracted him enough to put an end to the nervous ear tugging.

Curly Squirrelly was an Eastern Grey Squirrel, who despite his name was entirely black. He was called Curly due to the exaggerated curl in his tail, except when he ran. Then and only then was it straight, except for the tip which would still curl under slightly. The squirrel was a font of information. He knew everything and everyone who lived in the park. If you needed news, he was the next best thing to the *Tattler* newspaper or the SPN a.k.a. Stanley Park Network news on TV.

"Why are you over here? Is there any news of hatching yet?" Persimmon asked, looking out over the water and under the bridge towards Lost Lagoon.

"No, not yet," Curly answered around a mouthful of sunflower seed. "I'm just over here giving Queen Zoe, the swan queen, some time to herself to have her morning bath. She should be done by now."

"Hmmm," pondered Persimmon while watching the ducks paddling lazily on the pond. He wondered when the geese would arrive at the Goose Greens for their morning huddle.

"I wonder if Queen Zoe will share any of that special grain she gets from the Two Footers?" Curly mused mostly to himself. He turned to Persimmon. "What is on the agenda today? Do you think Queen Zoe will continue her stories about the Two Doors?" Curly asked Persimmon enthusiastically. The squirrel was nearly hopping up and down in his excitement.

"Not the Two Doors, Curly. You mean the Tudors. It's spelled T-U-D-O-R-S. And I'm sure if she has time, she will continue her story of Tudor times."
After all, the swans were royalty and knew all about the royalty of other places in the world. Curly and Persimmon loved the stories about a place named England and the kings, queens and

the royal court the best.

"Right! Tudors. History rocks!" Curly exclaimed earnestly.

Persimmon agreed. History was very interesting and it was one of the major reasons that Persimmon had discovered that there were other places in the world. It had started his thinking about travelling and surfing the world over. Someday he would write about all the places that for now he only explored in his mind.

He wondered how the swans knew all these things. He thought the swans were magnificent. There was also something mesmerizing about them. They were so graceful and tranquil that Persimmon always found himself in awe whenever he watched them gliding across the lagoon. It was one of the few times he wasn't in a rush. It was also one of the few times a fox could sneak up on him.

Persimmon shook his head. Just thinking of the swans had his brain gathering wool. He refocused his gaze and listened as Curly continued speaking.

"Anyways, if there was any hatching action, I would have announced it from the treetops before that Hector Noisy Fella Crow and his flock of crow pals knew what was happening!" Curly announced proudly. He swallowed the last of the sunflower seed and buried the husk in the soft earth at his feet. "Let's go!"

Persimmon grinned to himself. Everyone knew about the feud

Curly had going with the crows, except maybe for Hector himself. For as long as Persimmon could remember Curly was the first up in the morning and the last to bed at night. It was the only way to beat the crows to the food and the news. Curly Squirrelly also happened to be better connected to The Bird Network than the crows were, so news travelled faster to the squirrel than it did to the crows on any day. It was something the crows certainly did not appreciate.

Chapter Two

The squirrel and the hare scampered around the edges of the lagoon in the misty morning light. It was still quiet in the park and everyone was just waking up, but it wouldn't be long before a crowd had gathered around the swans' nest at Lost Lagoon. Everyone in the park was waiting for the Big Event. Even the Two Footers were buzzing with excitement.

Persimmon and Curly dashed through the tall grasses along the edge of the lagoon onto a waterlogged log so they could peer into the swans' nest. The nest was lined with the comfy stalks of dried reeds and lagoon plants. White feathers and down were carefully woven into the nest, making a cozy little bed for the single pale, bluish green egg nestled there safely. Queen Zoe Swan stood quietly in the nest, gazing intently into the still lagoon. She looked as if she had been stretching.

"Good morning, your Majesty," Persimmon greeted the swan with a bow. Curly did the same, nearly tipping himself off the log and into the water.

"Greetings Persimmon, Curly," the queen answered without taking her eyes from the water.

Persimmon wondered if she was staring at her reflection in the water's surface. If she was, Persimmon couldn't blame her, because she was beautiful indeed. She was a pristine white, her eyes jet black, yet soft with kindness. Her upper bill was a bright orange, the lower bill was black. There was a dainty black knob at the top of her bill that marked her as a Mute Swan.

"The egg is so beautiful," breathed Curly with wonder. His black eyes were as big as saucers as he looked at the egg. It was the only egg that had been laid this year at the lagoon, therefore it was very special. Persimmon thought it merely looked lonely sitting still and silent all by itself.

The birth of a Mute Swan was a huge deal in the park. So big that everyone called it the Big Event. For 36 days after the laying, they would all wait anxiously for the swans' egg to hatch. For the last 35 days, only King Arthur and Queen Zoe Swan seemed calm as they tended their egg tirelessly. Everyone else was waiting restlessly.

Once the egg finally hatched, everyone would relax. Everyone would be delighted to see the small bundle of grey with a black little beak, and black little legs that would emerge from the egg. The cygnet would hatch wet, wobbly, helpless, and oh, so very cute. Everyone would ooh and ah and gush excitedly over the new little prince or princess.

It wouldn't be long before the new Mama and Papa Swan would shoo everyone away so they wouldn't frighten the hatchling. The next time anyone saw the little one, it would be dry and fuzzy. It would be following its Mama and Papa upon the water. Or it would be riding comfortably on one of its parents' backs, or tucked under the safety of one of its parents' wings.

"How much longer will it be now, Queen Zoe?" Persimmon asked, balancing carefully on the log. He wished that Curly would stay still instead of fidgeting. It was making the log move unsteadily. If they weren't careful, they would both land in the lagoon.

"Do you think it will be a boy or a girl?" Persimmon asked next. He couldn't keep his curiosity from escaping. Even though he wanted to seem grown up in front of the Queen, he couldn't help it. He was after all, still a fairly young hare.

Queen Zoe smiled indulgently. Even though she was a very young queen, she was very patient and motherly. She cared for everyone who came to visit her at the lagoon.

"All is well and going as expected. It won't be long now, maybe a day or two at the most. I think it will be what it will be, boy or girl it will be a happy day indeed, as long as the hatchling is healthy. We will all be surprised," she answered, her voice regal and serene. "What do you think it will be?"

"I think it will be a swan for sure!" Persimmon exclaimed with a laugh, and Curly twittered behind him. Queen Zoe smiled wide.

"I think it will be a prince, your Majesty! A handsome prince!" Curly declared, jumping up and down on the log and forgetting for a moment where he was. The squirrel teetered when the log dipped gently, his arms wind milling franticly. Persimmon reached out a paw to steady him, even though his own balance wasn't quite steady.

"Perhaps," Queen Zoe said tranquilly, though she was trying not to laugh. Not wanting to laugh at Curly and hurt his feelings or make him embarrassed, she tucked a feather that was becoming untangled back into the nest. She couldn't help the corners of her bill curling upwards with a silent smile.

Persimmon looked out across Lost Lagoon towards the Jubilee Fountain. He thought he might take a swim over to the fountain if the spring day got warm. He dipped a toe from his hind leg into the water carefully and pulled it out quickly with a shiver.

The water was freezing! Maybe not today, he reconsidered.

"Where is the king today, Queen Zoe?" Persimmon asked, his whiskers quivering.

"He is across the way looking for any sign of mollusks and tender algae for me," Queen Zoe answered. Happy with the neatness of her nest, she gingerly sat on her single egg. Her feathers rustled and fluffed, and her head tipped downwards as her neck curved gracefully. She held her wings poised over her back. She looked very regal and graceful.

"I wouldn't worry about where King Arthur is, Persimmon. I would worry about where those raccoons are," Curly whispered. His little black eyes were fastened upon the Sleepy Willow Tree on the opposite bank of the lagoon. It was directly across from Queen Zoe's nest.

Suddenly there was a loud caw above them, and Persimmon, Curly, and Queen Zoe looked up at the sky. It was Hector Noisy Fella Crow, flying over the lagoon in small, tight circles. He spiraled downwards until he landed lightly upon the log next to Curly. The log bobbed up and down, and Hector grinned apologetically at Persimmon and Curly. Curly grabbed onto Persimmon for balance, and Persimmon stood upon the log like it was a surf board.

"Crows," Curly mumbled under his breath. "Be careful, Hector!"

"Ouch! Not so tight, Curly!" Persimmon objected in a loud

whisper. He was trying to pry Curly's arms from around his waist.

Hector was one of the abundant North Western Crows that lived in Stanley Park. He was the only crow that Curly actually sort of got along with, and that was only because Hector was good friends with Curly's mother. Hector was very fond of good manners and fancy dressing. He liked to wear a bow tie and was actually quite a distinguished gentleman who tried his best not to be rude, though he didn't always succeed.

Because of his preference for manners, Hector also tried not to be loud. He did not have much success with this either. It was just his nature to be loud. No matter how he tried his voice was blaring and sharp. Every time he spoke, it was hard not to hear him and wince. He was a crow after all.

"Raccoons! Raccoons! Raccoons!" Hector squawked noisily. "Raccoons are villains! Raccoons wear masks! Raccoons are tricksey! They disrupt the peace!" Considering how noisome Hector was, Persimmon thought that was a funny remark.

"Well, better out of sight for now, if I don't say so myself," a new voice chimed in, and a spry and spunky young skunk joined the group.

It was Penelope the Striped Skunk. Penelope was the size of a big house cat. She had a black body and two broad, white stripes down her back. Her bushy tail was edged with white, and she liked to swish it proudly back and forth. She had small black paws that were always dancing and springing with glee. Her face was very pretty and dainty with beautiful big, moss green eyes that were surrounded by a fluttery fringe of dark lashes. On her forehead there was a white starburst. She was the only skunk in the whole park with that white starburst, which made Penelope feel very special and very recognizable.

Penelope leaped onto the log from the bank of the lagoon. Curly squealed and jumped into the air, all his fur standing on end and his tail straight out. The squirrel landed on his belly, his hind legs grabbing the log on either side while his hands covered his eyes.

"Oh, Curly, you're so funny! Stop worrying, you won't fall in!" Penelope laughed mischievously. She started prancing back and forth along the log, bobbing and weaving as she did the "Walk Like an Egyptian" dance.

"Hi, Penelope," Persimmon greeted the newcomer. Hector bobbed his head from side to side. Curly was still covering his eyes.

"Hey, Persimmon! I saw the Raccoons messing about at the playground all last night. They were sliding down all the slides and swinging on the swings. I don't think we'll see them today. That should make you happy, Noisy Fella," Penny giggled, her little voice bright and sunny as always. With a quick move, Penelope flipped herself into a handstand. She made the log dip so that water sloshed over the top of the log, wetting Persimmon's and Hector's feet and Curly's belly.

"Eek! Eureka!" Curly squealed as the cold water nipped at his fur and the skin underneath. Persimmon finally just grabbed his tail and lifted him up, hind end first and dripping wet.

"Hello, Penny," Curly stammered with a shiver. Persimmon was helping him to stand slowly and regain his balance. Once standing, Curly began brushing off his fur. Penny was the only critter that couldn't ruffle Curly's fur. He had the hugest crush on the skunk and nothing she did, no matter how much mischief it caused, made Curly blink an eye.

"Any hatching action yet?" Penelope questioned, peering curiously at the nest trying to catch a peek under Queen Zoe.

"Nothing yet. Nothing for a day or two yet, most likely. All is quiet and still on the egg front," Curly informed Penny, happy to share the news.

"Speaking of disrupting the peace, Noisy Fella, why don't you dazzle us with some vocal stylings and sing the little egg a lullaby?" Penelope suggested with a gleam in her eye. "Singing it from right over the Sleepy Willow should be perfect. The sound will be just right from over there." The Sleepy Willow Tree also happened to be home to the Raccoons, who were probably sleeping the day away.

"Caw! Caw! Caw! Don't mind if I do," Hector agreed instantly, eager to sing. He loved singing. He would audition for *Canadian Idol* if crows were allowed. Too bad the songbirds wouldn't let him join their opera group. He was convinced he was an excellent singer. With a clumsy bow for the queen, Hector took flight, singing "Rock-a-Bye Baby" quite off key.

Penelope lifted a paw to wave at Hector, all her weight on one hand. Queen Zoe fluffed her feathers and closed her eyes, drifting off to sleep with the sound of Hector's voice trailing off into the distance. Persimmon wondered how she could sleep with the racket the crow was making.

"Well, boys, since there's no hatching action, what do you say we hop over to the playground before the mini Two Footers arrive and have some fun? There's some sweet clover growing over yonder that we can nibble on the way!" Penelope said, flipping herself back onto her hind legs. Dancing around Persimmon, she grabbed Curly's hands and danced a jig, ignoring the squirrel's squeaks of protest.

"That sounds like a good plan," Persimmon agreed, his tummy growling. Sweet clover sounded more than fine to him. "What do you say, Curly?"

"I think I'm good," Curly answered, sitting down with relief when Penelope released him. He exhaled mightily, puffing out his squirrelly cheeks.

"Alright, I'll see you later then. Are you sure you'll be okay?" Persimmon asked skeptically. Penelope stepped lightly around Persimmon again to get to the other end of the log. The log bobbed some more and Curly looked quite green in the face. "I'm sure. I'm going to relax right here and wait for my seasickness to go away," Curly half joked. "That way, I'll be right here if the egg hatches and I can be the very first to spread the news!"

"Alrighty, see you later," Persimmon replied, sidestepping Penny and hopping lightly off the log.

"Too-da-loo!" Penelope chimed out with a jaunty waggle of farewell with her fingers and a flirty bat of her eyelashes. She bent her knees and elbows as if to leap powerfully off the log and Curly cringed, but instead she stepped daintily off the edge of the log to the bank of the lagoon. Teasing Curly was so much fun. She blew a kiss over her shoulder for him.

Persimmon bowed and Penny bowed. "Your Majesty," they said together. They raced each other through the tall grass, disappearing towards Ceperley playground.

Curly exhaled mightily and settled down to wait. The log had stopped moving and finally he could relax. He had just started breathing calmly again when out of the blue the grasses parted with a loud rustle.

"Have I missed it? Have I missed the Big Event?" the voice was loud enough to be a shout. It was Benjamin Mole.

Once again Curly jumped into the air, startled beyond belief as the mole burst through the lagoon reeds. Curly landed on the log and unfortunately for him, the log started to spin in the water under Curly's feet. To stay on the log, Curly started to jog, and the log started to spin faster and faster until Curly was nearly sprinting.

Now as luck would or wouldn't have it, Benjamin happened to be very clumsy. He was even clumsier without his glasses, and wouldn't you know it, Benjamin had forgotten his glasses in his haste. Having trouble seeing where he was going, Ben tumbled head first off the bank. He grabbed for the log, hoping to avoid falling into the water. He managed to grab the log, but bumped it quite hard, which finally toppled Curly straight into the lagoon. Into the cold water Curly went with a loud sploosh, splash and a loud howl.

"Oh dear," whispered a worried Benjamin. Now he'd done it.

"Help! Help! I can't swim! I can't see!" cried the panicked squirrel. His little head was covered by his wet tail as he flailed up and down in the water. He doggy paddled frenziedly, his attempts at swimming carrying him farther out into the deeper water of the lagoon, sputtering and coughing all the while.

"Curly, you're going the wrong way!" wailed Benjamin, clinging desperately to the log.

Awoken by the ruckus, Queen Zoe's eyes snapped open and she stood abruptly. Taking in the situation, the queen sprang into action. First, she lifted Benjamin up out of the water and onto the bank of the lagoon. She looked out over the water, dismayed to see Curly splashing even farther out into the lagoon.

"Mink in the water! Mink in the water!" cried Curly with alarm. He felt an underwater plant tug at his feet and began to squall in earnest. "Oh goodness! I'm going to be eaten and then I'm going to sink!" All his panicked paddling had taken him far off into the lagoon quite quickly. At the rate he was going, he would make it to Jubilee Fountain, which was practically way over at the other end of Lost Lagoon.

Queen Zoe wondered if Curly had even realized yet that he was swimming, even if he believed he wasn't or couldn't. She wished he would just calm down and try to float on his back. How unfortunate that land animals panicked so much at the thought of being in the water. It really was quite soothing to be in it.

Without another thought, Queen Zoe stepped into the water and quickly paddled out after Curly. She was determined to rescue the frightened squirrel from the jaws of the imagined mink.

Her single egg was left all alone, undefended in the nest.

Chapter Three

Persimmon and Penelope stood at the top of the slide nibbling on the last of the sweet clover. Persimmon rubbed his hands together then smoothed his whiskers. His ears twitched.

"Well, who's going to go first?" Persimmon asked Penelope with a grin.

"You go first!" Penelope said with a giggle and gave Persimmon a push down the slide.

"Woohoo!" Persimmon exclaimed with glee all the way down to the bottom.

Penelope clapped her little hands, jumping up and down. Maybe the raccoons and the mini Two Footers were on to something. The playground was so much fun. They would have to come here more often.

"Weehoo!" Penelope hooted, and down the slide she went.

Persimmon had already run around to the bottom of the slide stairs and started to climb, eagerly making his way back up to the top. He was just about to go down again when Penelope yelled up at him.

"Wait for me! Don't go down 'til I get there. Then we can slide down together at the same time like a train! Woo woo!"

"Okay!" Persimmon answered with a chuckle. This was a great way to start the day. Maybe he would start everyday with sweet clover for breakfast and a slide or two before school. But wait — today was Saturday so there was no school! Persimmon's heart began to pound with excitement.
Since it was still early spring, the waters of English Bay would be even colder than the lagoon. Braving the waves and trying out his new surf board would have to wait. But, since today was Saturday, there was a good chance that he could convince his

dad to take him to see the Hollow Tree! He'd ask Curly to call him if the egg looked like it was close to hatching so he could run back and not miss the Big Event. Then later on he could stake out the mysterious lights. What a day this was going to be!

Persimmon peered down at Penelope who was preening and smoothing her ruffled fur. Well, at least she thought it was ruffled. She always thought it was ruffled when it usually wasn't. She was very proud of her glossy black fur. She was even prouder of the pair of stripes that went down her back. She spent a lot of time making sure not one white hair was out of place. Penelope was definitely a girly girl, but she was still a lot of fun.

Suddenly there was a sound in the distance that caught Persimmon's attention. His long ears twitched back and forth, trying to discover the source of the sound. Just then, Penelope arrived at the top of the slide, a huge smile on her face.

"Let's go!" Penelope exclaimed. She put her hands on Persimmon's shoulders and tried to turn him around so they could go down the slide.

"Wait, Penelope. Listen. Do you hear something?" Penelope tilted her head, trying to locate the sound. She was very serious now.

"Nope, nothing. What do you hear?"

Persimmon looked across the field and road, trying to see through the trees to the lagoon. The sun was very bright now and Persimmon raised his paw to shield his eyes. He squinted into the distance, but he couldn't make anything out. The sound, however, was very clear to him now.

"Mink in the water! Mink in the water!" was the cry Persimmon heard.

"It's Curly! There's something going on at the lagoon. Let's go! Hurry!" Persimmon grabbed Penelope's hand and jumped onto the slide, skidding down on his long feet like he was surfing.

Without wasting any time, they dashed across the field, the road and the Goose Greens where the geese liked to hang out. They made their way down the path that led to the lagoon, past Persimmon's and Gilly's house. They were running as fast as they could. Breathless, they burst through the tall grasses at the edge of the lagoon near the swans' nest and scampered back onto the log. Benjamin Mole was there, a worried expression on his face.

Benjamin Mole was a Coast Mole. He wasn't very large, maybe a little larger than Curly Squirrelly. He had beautiful thick, velvety black short fur. His tail was hairless and not very long, and his nose was long and pointed and hairless, too. His feet were also bare of fur. His front paws were much larger than his back paws as he used them for digging. They were wide and spade shaped and very strong with very long nails. He usually stayed underground unless something very exciting was going on above ground, like the expected hatching of a precious swan egg.

Benjamin's ears weren't visible on his head, but they were there nonetheless. He had tiny black eyes and he had a hard time seeing anything unless he had his glasses. At this moment, those glasses were not on Benjamin's face. Persimmon knew he wouldn't get much of an answer, but he had to ask anyway.

"What happened?" Persimmon asked in a rush. He was very worried and it was very clear in his voice.

"I'm not sure," Benjamin stuttered. He turned to peer at Persimmon, one tiny eye closed and the other tiny eye open. "I forgot my glasses because I was in a hurry. I think I knocked Curly into the lagoon and a mink is after him. Queen Zoe lifted me onto the bank here, but I'm not sure where she is now. What shall we do if a mink is snapping at Curly's toes? I can't see without my glasses."

Persimmon had been listening intently to Benjamin's version of events while his keen eyes scanned the lagoon. He could

see Queen Zoe gliding smoothly and calmly through the water towards them. Persimmon could just make out a little patch of wet black fur tucked safely onto Queen Zoe's back. Relieved, Persimmon turned back to the agitated mole.

"It's okay, Benjamin. Curly is safe. Queen Zoe is bringing him back right now," Persimmon said soothingly, patting Benjamin's shoulder. Just then, Persimmon noticed the nest. It was with a sick feeling in the pit of his stomach that Persimmon had to ask the important question.

"Umm, Benjamin, where is the egg?"

Chapter Four

Penelope and Benjamin stared at Persimmon with alarm. No one said a word. All three heads turned to watch as Queen Zoe, with Curly tucked safely on her back, sailed gracefully towards the nest and the log where they stood. Then with sheer horror, the heads of mole, skunk and hare turned to stare at the empty nest.

"Oh no! Oh no! Oh no! This can't be happening!" cried Penelope. Her eyes were glued to the empty nest. "What are we going to tell Queen Zoe? She'll be devastated! What will we tell King Arthur? Oh no," Penelope whispered this last little bit, quite horrified. Tears welled in the outside corners of her eyes. She put her hands to the sides of her face and her brows puckered in a worried frown.

"This can't be happening," Persimmon said, his own eyes looking at the nest. He felt filled with pain and sorrow. What were they going to say to the king and queen? Their precious egg was missing. No matter what was said, it was going to break their hearts.

"What do you mean where is the egg, Persimmon? Where is the egg? Isn't it in the nest? Shouldn't it be in the nest?" Benjamin Mole asked, his voice rising with alarm.

"Shhhhhh!" Persimmon cautioned his friend, motioning with his paws for Ben to keep it down. Persimmon looked over his shoulder towards the lagoon. Queen Zoe and Curly were almost upon them.

"What do you mean where is the egg?" Ben repeated in a loud, harsh whisper. "I thought it was in the nest safe and sound."

"Well it's not," Persimmon stated. This was a big disaster. "The egg is gone."

"G-g-g-g-gone! Oh no, no, no!" wailed Benjamin.

"Shhhhhh!" both Persimmon and Penelope shooshed in harmony.

"What are we going to tell Queen Zoe?" Benjamin asked, his voice nothing more than a horrified whisper.

"Yes, Persimmon. What will we say?" Penelope asked. Persimmon had never seen Penelope without the twinkle in her eyes.

"Don't worry, neither of you. I will tell Queen Zoe. It will be okay." Persimmon soothed. He squeezed Ben's shoulder and Penelope's hand. He stood facing the lagoon, waiting and watching as Queen Zoe gently deposited a damp and ruffled Curly on the bank.

"Oh, your Majesty, thank you, thank you, thank you! I can't

thank you enough! I can't even begin to think —" Curly Squirrelly was interrupted by Queen Zoe.

"Don't worry about it, Curly," Queen Zoe reassured the squirrel. "It is my job to make sure no harm comes to any who live within the park." She patted Curly on his head gently with her beak.

"Queen Zoe, there is some very troubling news —" Persimmon started to say at the exact same moment that Queen Zoe stepped onto her nest. Persimmon's voice fell away and he became silent. There was no need to say anything.

Queen Zoe stood looking down at her empty nest. All was still and a terrible silence filled the air.

"Where is my egg?" Queen Zoe asked of them, her voice was very flat, almost without hope.

"We're not quite sure, your Majesty," Persimmon answered solemnly. "Penelope and I heard Curly hollering so we came back as fast as we could. We noticed the egg was missing when we got here. I don't think Ben saw anything because he wasn't wearing his glasses."

"W-well, I didn't see anything, but I did hear something," Ben stammered uncertainly.

"What did you hear, Benjamin? Quick you must tell me!" Queen Zoe urged. She approached Ben and put her head down right in front of his own head. They were beak to snout. Benjamin's long nose quivered.

"I'm not sure —" Ben said uncertainly.

"Try and remember, Ben. This is important." Queen Zoe's voice was low and urgent. She knew she couldn't push him too hard. Mole didn't do well under pressure and he might not be able to tell her what happened if he became flustered. And she needed to know what he had heard. Ben's mole ears might not be visible, but he did have very, very acute hearing.

"I heard Curly fall into the lagoon…then I heard you paddle after him, your Majesty, and then…I think I heard some whispering and then I heard some rustling. Yeah! I did! That's it!" Benjamin beamed a wide smile at his friends.

"That's great, Benjamin," Queen Zoe said, her voice determined. "I must call King Arthur and the other swans so we can start searching."

With that, Queen Zoe lifted her graceful head and let out a long, mournful call across the lagoon. She followed it with three quick and loud bursts of sound. She held her head high, waiting for an answer. Persimmon, Penelope, Benjamin and Curly all held their breaths, and then a call echoed back to them from across the lagoon.

"King Arthur is coming," Queen Zoe translated for them. "Wait here while I go and gather the ducks to help search."

"Yes, your Majesty," the four furry friends answered, bowing their heads respectfully. Queen Zoe stepped deftly into the water and swam off faster than anyone had ever seen her swim before.

"This is all my fault," Curly whispered sadly. He hung his head in shame and hugged his wet tail to his chest. His usually boisterous nature had completely vanished.

Persimmon went up to his friend and put an arm around his shoulder to comfort him. "It's not your fault, Curly. Sometimes things happen and we don't know why." Penelope and Benjamin nodded encouragement at Persimmon's statement.

"But if I hadn't panicked when I fell into the water, none of this would've happened," Curly whispered dejectedly, still blaming himself.

"It's not all your fault, Curly. If I hadn't forgotten my glasses, or scared you, you wouldn't have fallen into the water to begin with," Benjamin countered, placing a hand on Curly's arm.

"Let's not play the blame game, you guys," Persimmon said firmly. "What we need to do is find that egg." Persimmon's voice was determined and his heather colored eyes simmered with resolve.

"But that's impossible. This park is huge. We'll never find it," Curly moaned.

"Don't be pessimistic, Curly," Penelope admonished. "I know that look on Persimmon's face. He has a plan!" Penelope hopped up and down excitedly.

"That I do, Penelope. But I'm going to need all the help I can get." Persimmon turned to Curly and took both his shoulders in his paws. He gave the little squirrel a gentle shake.

"Nothing is impossible, Curly," Persimmon said fervently. "I am a Snowshoe Hare living in Stanley Park when everyone knows that Snowshoe Hares don't live in Stanley Park. Me being here, that is an impossibility, yet here I am. Nothing is impossible, Curly. Remember that."

Curly straightened his shoulders and lifted his head. He took a deep breath. "I'll remember."

Persimmon nodded at him, satisfied that Curly wouldn't give up.

"I have a plan. We are going to find that egg. Who's with me?" Persimmon put his paw out in front of him, looking at each of his friends in turn.

"I am!" Penelope answered enthusiastically, and placed her own elegant paw over Persimmon's.

"So am I!" Benjamin piped in and put his large, spade shaped paw over Penelope's.

"I'm in, too," Curly said very seriously. He placed his own little paw over Ben's.

Persimmon's ears twitched and his whiskers quivered. With a gleam in his eye, he put his other paw on top of everyone else's. "Let's do this!"

Chapter Five

Hector Noisy Fella was silent for once, though he was bobbing his head back and forth, up and down. More Stanley Park critters had arrived at the nest. The crow was eyeing everyone but Persimmon, Queen Zoe and King Arthur suspiciously. The ducks had ceased their constant quacking and flapping and sat still on the water around the swans' nest. The other four swans who lived at the lagoon had joined the group as well, all ready to offer their help to the king and queen. The geese were still absent — that was very strange indeed! No one had seen even a single one as of yet at the Goose Greens, the field by the pond where they liked to hang out.

Persimmon wished there was more time to gather a larger search party, but this would just have to do for know. It was time to put his plan into action. As soon as King Arthur was done organizing everyone into groups, Persimmon would share his idea.

King Arthur was the most majestic Mute Swan on the lagoon. He was the biggest and the oldest swan. He was wise and fair and very brave. He was also very intimidating to everyone who lived at Stanley Park for no other reason than that he carried himself with a great authority. He was a very good king, well loved and respected by all. He was addressing the other two pairs of swans in his low, deep voice.

"William and Matilda, you take the north and south eastern areas of the lagoon. Jasper and Sorcha, you will scour the north and south western corners of the lagoon. I already have the Beavers exploring the grasses surrounding the lagoon," ordered King Arthur firmly.

The swans nodded silently, bowing their elegant heads. As one fleet and graceful group, they left the gathering to go and scour the lagoon.

"Ducks, you will dive the pond beyond and under the bridges. Leave not one square inch of mud or water overlooked," continued the King.

"Hector," the King paused for a moment. "You, your brothers, sisters and cousins will flock to the skies and search the park from high above. Report anything at all suspicious back to the queen or myself. We will stay near the nest and investigate the water and grasses around it. Let us hope we can find our egg before too much time passes."

"Absolutely anything suspicious! Rats and raccoons, rats and raccoons! Suspicious for sure! Caw!" Hector exclaimed in his clamorous voice. He flapped his wings and lifted himself into the sky, eager to start his searching; though he wasn't eager to hang out with the other crows and their continual squabbling.

Queen Zoe was trying bravely to hold back her tears. Seeing this, King Arthur swam up to his Queen and touched his head to hers. He placed his wing around her in comfort. Persimmon could not hear what he whispered to her. Persimmon decided now was the time to speak up and offer his help and the help of his friends. He cleared his throat.

"Pardon me, your Majesty, King Arthur. I would like to offer some help."

King Arthur turned to Persimmon who still stood with his friends upon the log.

"What do you think you children can do to help, young Persimmon?" the king asked kindly, though his voice sounded weary.

"I know someone with a highly sensitive nose. With your permission, I would like to bring him to the nest to search for clues," Persimmon requested.

"I don't see what harm it could do," Queen Zoe stated hopefully. "We need to try everything we can." She looked to King Arthur for agreement.

Unable to deny his queen anything, King Arthur nodded, showing his support for his queen's decision. "You have our permission, Persimmon. We are grateful for your help."

"We are glad to be of service, your Majesty," Persimmon answered, eager to put his plan into action. Penelope, Curly and Benjamin all breathed a sigh of relief.

"Queen Zoe," the four friends said and bowed to the queen.

Next they bowed to the king. "King Arthur," they murmured. The royal couple inclined their heads. Then without another word, both swans dived under the water, hoping the search for their lost egg wouldn't be in vain.

Persimmon, Penelope, Curly and Benjamin scampered off the log and headed to Persimmon's house.

* * *

The four friends gathered inside of Persimmon's barn shaped shed in the back yard. Persimmon didn't want Gilly to overhear their conversation. He didn't want his parent's to worry either about what he was planning to do just yet.

"Benjamin, I need you to tell me if you have any idea who it could be that took the egg based on the sounds you heard."

"Sorry, Persimmon, I have no idea," Ben answered, scratching his head.

"Okay, no worries. I need you to go underground and see if there is any news. Somebody might have heard or seen something we haven't. If you find out anything, call me on my Blackberry."

"Your blackberry?" Benjamin asked, puzzled. Now why would Persimmon want him to call him on a piece of fruit?

"My cell phone. It's called a Blackberry. What's your home phone number? I'll call you so you have my number." Persimmon took out his Blackberry from the pocket in the back of his tie. Ben must be the only critter in the park who didn't have a cell phone of some sort. Maybe it was because the reception underground wasn't very good.

"Now," Persimmon continued, "if I'm not back by 6 o'clock tonight, you'll need to tell my parents that I've been in a bit of trouble. Penelope and Curly will come to see them and tell them not to worry."

"Okay," Benjamin agreed uncertainly. "Just what are you planning to do?"

"I can't say yet. I don't want anyone to start worrying already," Persimmon said with a wink. "I'll catch you later."

"Alright," Ben said skeptically. With a last look at Persimmon, he dove into the bushes and Persimmon could hear him scrabbling in the dirt starting to dig.

"Well, musketeers," Persimmon turned to Curly and Penelope. "All for one…"

"And one for all!" Curly and Penelope finished enthusiastically.

"Come on. We need to get to the beach by 8 o'clock this morning, or my plan won't work."

The friends scampered out from the underbrush and through the park, making their way quickly to the beach. Luckily the park was still very quiet at this hour. That was a good thing because the last thing they needed was a bunch of Two Footers interfering with their plan and slowing them down. They reached the Sea Wall pathway and dashed across it. They jumped down over the low brick wall and hid amongst the pile of old logs piled up on the sand at the base of the wall.

Persimmon peeked out through the logs over the beach. Earlier that morning, before the swans' egg had gone missing, Persimmon had thought it was going to be a beautiful sunny day. Now, looking out over English Bay and the choppy grey water and the dark clouds over head, Persimmon knew the day was going to be miserable. It was almost as if Mother Nature herself was weeping over the loss of the precious egg.

Persimmon's keen eyes scanned the beach, hoping he would find what he was looking for. If it started to pour with rain before he could complete his plan, everything would be ruined. Fortunately for the swans, the threat of rain didn't stop the woman and her dog from enjoying their usual morning at the beach.

"What are we looking for?" Penelope asked Persimmon in a breathless whisper. Curly stood on the other side of him, trying to scramble onto the log to see what they were seeing.

"See there? That lady and her German Shepherd?" pointed out Persimmon.

"Yes," both Curly and Penelope said at once. Their voices were filled with doubt.

"Well, they are part of my plan," Persimmon declared bravely.

"Are you out of your mind?" Curly nearly screeched. "You mean, Danger over there?"

"What exactly are you thinking, Persimmon? Putting yourself in danger isn't going to solve anything." Penelope was incredulous. This was definitely a hare brained scheme.

"Have some faith. Believe this can work and it will. Trust me," Persimmon beseeched earnestly.

"Okay, so what are we going to do?" the doubting pair asked reluctantly.

Persimmon's ears twitched and his whiskers quivered. He smiled impishly.

"That is Mercutio and his owner. Every day during the week, between 8 am to exactly 9 am, they come to the beach so the lady can do something called Tai Chi and then some meditation, for exactly one hour. Mercutio lays on the sand watching his owner, bored as bored can be. His owner is so focused on what she's doing that she isn't focusing on Mercutio."

"And why is she not concerned about what Danger himself is doing?" Curly questioned Persimmon.

"She trusts that Mercutio is just going to sit and wait patiently." Persimmon was staring intently at the dog. Curly and Penelope could feel his excitement.

"Okay, so where does all this fit in?" Penelope asked, knowing she wasn't going to like the answer.

"We are going to get Mercutio to chase me," Persimmon said with a smile.

Chapter Six

Both Penelope's and Curly's mouth hung open with surprise. Persimmon put his paws under their chins and closed their mouths for them at the same time. The sound of the surf and the seagulls flying overhead were the only sounds to be heard.

"Curly, you are going to go up to Mercutio and get his attention," Persimmon directed, laying out the plan.

Curly gulped, truly alarmed. "Just how close, exactly?"

"Just close enough to get his attention, but not close enough for him to catch you," Persimmon reassured with a grin. "Once you have his attention, run back to the logs as fast as you can."

Curly stared at the large canine.

Curly was certain that he was a German Shepherd with a little dash of monster mixed in there somewhere. Mercutio was a very big, and what the Two Footers would call, a very beautiful dog. His coat was a golden and mahogany color everywhere except along his back, which was black and sleek. His tail was long and plumed, very fancy indeed. He had big, brown, intelligent eyes that Curly knew saw everything.

The dog had big pointy ears that looked like they heard everything. He had huge paws at the ends of long, powerful legs that most likely could run very fast. And when the dog yawned, well, he showed off huge teeth that could make short work of a little squirrel like Curly.

Curly shuddered. This was not his idea of a good plan. Oh, no!

"O-k-k-aaay," Curly agreed despite his fear. He was still watching Mercutio with wide, nervous eyes.

"Penelope, before Curly gets to the logs, you are going to intercept Mercutio and get him to stop. You are going to tell him I have an offer for him that he won't be able to refuse."

"Alrighty," Penelope replied, gathering her courage and regaining her spryness. She rubbed her hands together.

"Let's do it," Persimmon instructed.

Curly took a deep breath and dashed out from the safety of the logs and across the sand before his little bit of courage failed him. He came to a skidding halt, splayed out on all fours in front of the German Shepherd. Golden grains of gritty sand sprayed across the dog's wet nose. The dog sneezed and rose into a sitting position, shaking the sand from his snout and rubbing his face with one of his huge paws.

Curly squeaked and chattered at the dog, jumping into the air when the dog shifted to a sitting position. Before Curly's body hit the beach, he was turning around and running as fast as his squirrelly legs could carry him. He ran, sand pelting Mercutio in the face as he made his way back to the safety of the logs.

Just when Curly thought he'd find himself in the jaws of the canine as a doggy snack, Penelope ran past him to intervene. Curly leaped at the logs and dived headfirst to safety.

Penelope charged at the approaching canine. She did a cartwheel and a flip and landed on her front paws, facing the dog with a daring smile on her face. Her hind legs were in the air, her body steady and curved over her head. Her plumed tail was poised, and she was prepared to aim and fire if she needed to. Now it was Mercutio's turn to come to a skidding halt on the sand. The last thing he wanted was to get sprayed by a skunk.

"Peace Mercutio, I will not spray you if you behave," Penelope warned calmly.

"Peace to you, Skunk. I will not bite you. Why are you and your squirrelly friend teasing me this morning?" Mercutio eyed Penelope warily.

"Well, I have a friend who wishes to speak with you. He has an offer you cannot refuse," replied Penelope.

"And just who is this friend of yours?" asked Mercutio curiously.

"My name is Persimmon. I need your nose," Persimmon answered, emerging from behind the safety of the logs. Curly peeked out from behind Persimmon, intrigued despite his apprehension.

"You need my nose?" Mercutio asked, confused by the strange request.

"Yes. We have lost something extremely important and we don't have a lot of time to find it. I can't think of any other way to find it quickly," stated the brave hare.

"Well, I suppose I could help you," the dog mused out aloud, looking back over his shoulder at his owner. "But I will get scolded if I leave the beach."

"I am sure that your owner —"

"My person," Mercutio corrected Persimmon politely.

"Your person will not mind if you help us. Do not bark and you will not worry her. I will make sure you are back before long. And in appreciation for your help, I will let you chase me." Finished with his proposal, Persimmon waited patiently for an answer. Dogs could never refuse to chase small, fluffy critters.

Mercutio frowned. "I do not bark, little rabbit. I have the blood of the noble Malamute within my veins. Malamutes are too dignified to go barking their heads off like nincompoops." Mercutio puffed out his chest with pride. "If I get scolded, it will not be because of my barking." He decided not to mention that he preferred howling, and that's what he got scolded for — especially if it was late at night or early in the morning or a full moon.

"I knew he was more than just a German Shepherd," Curly added from behind Persimmon's back. "Just look at his fluffy, wispy fur around his belly, legs, chest and ears! Danger is part fluffy monster! I knew it!"

Mercutio raised a brow at the squirrel. Curly squeaked and hid behind Persimmon once more.

"I will help you, rabbit, even if I don't get to chase you. I'd rather chase the squirrel, though," Mercutio teased, grinning widely and letting his tongue loll out from behind his teeth.

A horrified squeal erupted from behind Persimmon, and Mercutio and Penelope chuckled. Persimmon couldn't help grinning. Persimmon and Mercutio shook paws. Despite his large size, Mercutio was a very gentle and friendly dog.

"Well, I am a hare, not a rabbit," Persimmon corrected Danger. "I think Curly has had enough of being chased for one day," Persimmon said with an apologetic smile for Curly. "Just promise not to bite me, Mercutio. I'm rather fond of myself," Persimmon requested courteously.

"Just remember to run fast then, Persimmon Hare," teased Mercutio.

Persimmon, Penelope and Curly stared aghast at the dog.

"Just kidding" Mercutio chuckled, giving them another of his wide, doggy grins. He stood up, bouncing excitedly on the sandy beach. His tail wagged with joy.

"So I'll give you a head start, Persimmon. Three seconds," Mercutio announced, ready to give chase.

"We stop at the stone bridge. I'll yell home free. Deal?" Persimmon demanded, making sure his Blackberry was tucked safely inside the pocket at the back of his tie.

"Deal! One, two, three!" growled Danger in sheer glee.

And they were off in a mad dash, leaving Penelope and Curly to catch up to them. The two friends watched after Persimmon, not entirely okay with this plan. Yet they believed Persimmon was fast enough to outrun the dog. He was already a little white dot far off in the distance, running as fast as his Snowshoe feet would carry him.

Hopefully the dog didn't get carried away and forget that Persimmon wasn't breakfast. Penelope looked back at the dog's person doing her strange, silent movements on the beach. She would never understand Two Footers.

"Do you think we can trust Danger?" Curly echoed Penelope's thoughts. She thought it was hilarious that Curly called Mercutio Danger. She hoped he wasn't right, though.

"Well, if we can't trust Danger — I mean, Mercutio, I'll have to spray the dickens out of him. He'll smell so bad that no one will be able to stand him," she sniggered.

Chapter Seven

"What do you need me to find?" asked Mercutio Danger.

Persimmon and Mercutio had reached the stone bridge. Persimmon had hopped up on the stone railing of the bridge and looked out over the lagoon. In the distance, he could see the swans searching back and forth.

The chase had been very close. Persimmon was still catching his breath from fright as much as from exertion. Mercutio had gotten so close that he had butted Persimmon's cotton tail with his wet nose, propelling the hare forward. Persimmon's heart had skipped a beat, thinking that if this dog wasn't trustworthy, it could have been the snap of teeth he felt instead of a cold nose.

"See those swans over there? The swans by the nest?" Persimmon answered, pointing over to Queen Zoe and King Arthur. Mercutio stood up on his hind legs, draping his front paws upon the stone bridge railing next to Persimmon. The canine was still panting a little. Persimmon didn't feel so bad at being a bit winded himself now.

"Yes, I see them," Mercutio licked the sea salt off his lips and resumed panting. Persimmon wondered if it was just a dog thing to do, or if Mercutio thought swans might be tasty.

"They are our king and queen and they have lost their egg. If I'm being completely honest, I think someone has stolen it. I need your nose to help me find who took it. We find them, we find the egg," remarked Persimmon. He watched Danger keenly to see that the dog understood the urgency of the job in hand.

"Ah, I see. So technically, I'm helping you find two things. Not just one," Mercutio pointed out. He was always one to barter and he could do his math!

"Technically, yes, I suppose you are right," agreed Persimmon. After a moment he said, "I guess that means I owe you another chase then?"

"If you insist," Mercutio quipped happily.

"What do you mean another chase?" queried Curly sharply.

He and Penelope had just arrived at the stone bridge. Penelope eyed Persimmon critically, looking for any sign of injury. Persimmon thought he heard her mumble, "Lucky, Danger," under her breath. Mercutio must have heard her because he gave another one of his doggy grins and rolled his eye back at the skunk. Penelope smiled innocently at the dog.

"Well, technically he is helping us find two things. So technically I owe him two chases. It's only fair," Persimmon explained.

"Well, it's your tail," complained Curly. He still didn't quite
trust Mercutio. Persimmon couldn't quite blame him. He'd
never heard of a dog that didn't love to chase squirrels. Maybe
Mercutio would prove to be the exception — or would he?

"Well, let's go down to the nest," Mercutio decided. He took his
front paws off the stone railing and began heading across the
bridge towards the lagoon. "I'll see if I can pick up the sent of
the egg first. Then I'll look for the smell that doesn't belong."

Squirrel, skunk and hare followed the dog over the bridge. They
made a companionable group, the four of them walking side by
side. Even Curly had seemed to have forgotten for the moment
that he was wary of dogs. He was, however, the farthest away,
walking as he was next to Penelope, who was walking next to
Persimmon. Persimmon walked next to Mercutio, absorbed by
the prospect of chasing down the scent.

"I suppose you should tell the swans we're coming," Mercutio
suggested. "I wouldn't want to get pecked. I have a friend who
got pecked and was once chased pretty bad by a goose. Scared
the living daylights out of my poor pal. He has bad dreams now
about flocks of geese coming after him." Mercutio's tone was
extremely serious, but Persimmon thought he heard Curly giggle.

"Good idea," agreed Persimmon. "Curly, run ahead and tell the
king and queen we're on our way."

"Will do!" Curly squeaked. It was obvious he was relieved to have something to do that would take him away from the dog for now. The squirrel ran off to warn the swans and most likely any other water fowl that were close by.

When Persimmon, Penelope and Mercutio arrived at the nest, it was with cautious steps. Even though everyone knew a dog was visiting, Persimmon and Mercutio thought it would be best if their arrival was as calm as possible. Who knew what would happen if a big dog came bounding out of the bushes. Bedlam and confusion and disaster most likely, thought Persimmon. And goodness knew that they didn't need any more problems today.

Persimmon bowed. Penelope curtsied, which by the way, Persimmon thought was odd because she never curtsied. She always bowed. Oh, well. She was probably trying to impress Mercutio. Mercutio had decided to offer a bow of sorts, as well. He had bent a front leg beneath him, the other leg extended in front of him, and dipped his head elegantly. Very impressive, thought Persimmon. No wonder Penelope was being fancy.

"Your Majesties," greeted Persimmon. Penelope and Mercutio mumbled the same greeting. "This is Mercutio German Shep-herd —"

"Malamute Cross, your Majesties," Mercutio interrupted with a sideways glance at Persimmon. Mercutio it seemed had many names.

"Ahem," Persimmon cleared his throat. "Yes, Malamute Cross.

He has agreed to help us find the egg."

King Arthur approached his visitor, coming up out of the water and standing upon his large nest. He seemed to tower over the dog, who still had his head bent politely. After a moment of observation, King Arthur seemed pleased with what he made of his strange guest. The king stepped back, seeming more comfortable. It was then that Persimmon realized that the king had seemed larger than usual because he had puffed up his feathers and stood as tall as he ever had. He had been assessing the dog, trying to figure out whether or not the canine was really friend or foe. Obviously the king decided that the dog really was friendly. That should make Curly feel safer.

"Thank you for helping us, Mercutio German Shepherd Malamute Cross," the king said regally.

"Yes," said Queen Zoe gently. "Thank you. Please rise. What do you need from us?"

Mercutio first stood then sat down immediately. He did not want to make anyone nervous by reminding them he stood like a wolf and therefore was related.

"Well, first I need to catch the scent of the egg," Mercutio explained. "Then I need to eliminate smells that belong in the nest. Then just to be safe, I need to identify the scent of everyone present. Hopefully I'll be able to single out the scent that seems suspicious."

"Whatever you need, Mercutio German Shepherd Malamute Cross," agreed Queen Zoe.

"Please, just call me Mercutio," he said humbly.

"Mercutio, then," said Queen Zoe. "Go ahead."

Mercutio stood and gingerly walked over to the nest, nose to the ground. The only sound anyone heard was the loud sniffing noise Mercutio's nose made as he tried to find the scent of the egg. Without a word or looking at anyone, Mercutio continued to sniff the nest. His eyes were locked on it, absorbing everything around him as his nose covered every inch of the nest. Every time a downy feather got stuck to his nose, Mercutio would sneeze, blow out loudly then continue right on sniffing. Everyone waited silently and expectantly.

"Well, I believe I've identified the egg," Mercutio announced. There was an audible sigh of relief from everyone gathered. "Now I need to identify the scent of the parents to match it to what I smell in the nest." He looked at Queen Zoe awkwardly. Queen Zoe looked at her husband before stepping forward, her wings outspread. Carefully, Mercutio placed his nose against the queen's feathers. He sniffed delicately and respectably.

"Mmhmm," he said to himself. "Sire," Mercutio looked at King Arthur. The king stepped forward, subjecting himself to being identified by the canine's nose.

"Alright," Mercutio said. "There is a scent in the nest that I don't recognize. It isn't water fowl, so I don't have to smell the ducks or the other swans or water birds. There was another bird here, but only briefly and not near the egg smell. I already know what Persimmon smells like, and Penelope, so I don't have to put my nose in either of your fur coats." Penelope smirked as Mercutio continued. "There is a scent that smells like dirt?"

"That would be Benjamin Mole," Persimmon answered Mercutio.

"Alright. That leaves one more scent I need to figure out." Mercutio turned mischievous eyes upon Curly and the squirrel shrank with trepidation. He took a deep breath and stepped towards the dog.

"If you must," Curly said, knowing it was very important. "We must find the egg, we must find the egg," Curly repeated to himself out aloud.

Mercutio bounded over to Curly and shoved his nose into the squirrel's belly. Curly was tackled to the ground with a squeal that turned into a round of giggles as Mercutio tickled him, ruffling his black fur.

"Alright," declared Mercutio. "I've got it. I'm going to follow the scent."

Mercutio put his nose to the ground and diligently followed an invisible trail only he could make out. He moved quickly, moving away from the nest and through the grasses that surrounded the lagoon. He followed the scent to the stone bridge, stopping first at one side of the walkway. He snuffled in the tall grasses at the base of the bridge but didn't step onto it. Instead he walked to the other stone rail and sniffed around in the shrubbery growing there. He followed his nose under the bridge to the water's edge. Persimmon, Penelope, Curly, the swans and a gaggle of ducks trailed after him. He lifted his head.

"It goes into the water, two similar but slightly different scents. I'll pick it up on the other side. Persimmon, Penelope, Curly, hop on my back."

The three friends climbed onto Mercutio's back, holding on tight to his fur. Once on the other side of the narrow pond that wound its way from the lagoon and under the bridge, they slipped from Mercutio's back. The swans and ducks waded through the water behind them. They waited until Mercutio's diligent nose found the scent again and continued to follow him. He led them up the slight bank, through the dense grasses to the other end of the bridge. They walked across the end of the bridge to the shrubs and grass at its base.

Mercutio sniffed the same spot for a few moments then doubled back to the path that led away from the stone bridge to the other side of the lagoon. Everyone was silent, following Mercutio who was loping along rapidly now, his nose still to the ground. Finally he stopped at the base of the Sleepy Willow Tree that stood directly across from the king and queen's nest on the lagoon.

"The trail ends here!" Mercutio announced triumphantly. His tail was wagging with elation.

"I knew it!" cried Curly.

The willow tree was the home of two of the most mischievous raccoons in the whole of Stanley Park. Oscar and Felix Raccoon. They were bandits. They were rascals. And as Hector would say, they were tricksey.

"We will never get our egg back now," Queen Zoe nearly sobbed. King Arthur tucked her under his wide wing to comfort her. She turned to Mercutio. "I can't thank you enough, Mercutio. You are welcome to visit us whenever you like. We are in your debt."

"I am glad to help. There is no debt. Persimmon has already taken care of everything. I should get back, though. My time is up and it wouldn't do any good for the raccoons to notice me. They won't even come out to talk if I'm here. I hope you find your egg." Mercutio made another elegant bow. He then turned to Persimmon with a grim smile. "Until the next chase then, my friend. You know where to find me." And with that, Mercutio German Shepherd Malamute Cross bounded away back to the beach.

"Come, my dear," King Arthur coaxed his Queen. "We must return to the nest and gather as much down as we can. If the raccoons still have our egg, we will need something to trade for it. If I know those bandits, they won't even talk to us if we come empty handed." Queen Zoe nodded, her head bowed. "Thank you, Persimmon. You, too, Penelope and Curly. Come and see us when we have managed to retrieve our egg and have it settled safely in our nest once more."

"Yes, your Majesty," Persimmon replied. The three friends bowed in unison as the swans left. The ducks turned to follow the king and queen, waddling and quacking and complaining amongst themselves as they left.

"Well, now that we know where the egg is, we have to figure out a way to get it back." Persimmon was thinking out loud.

"What if those raccoons don't have the egg anymore?" Penelope asked worriedly.

"If I know those raccoons at all, I know they would never get rid of anything," replied Persimmon.

"Well, I think it's really unfair that the swans need to buy their own egg back. It's outrageous!" stormed Penelope.

"Well, as Hector would say, those Raccoons are villains!" Curly chimed in.

"Yes, they surely are. They are definitely tricksey," Penelope added, quite indignant.

"Which means we'll have to be just as tricksey if not more," Persimmon said cryptically. Penelope and Curly turned to look at Persimmon, eager for phase two of operation Save the Swan Egg.

Persimmon's ears twitched and his whiskers quivered.

"Speaking of Hector, we need to find him. We're going to need him to do some spying for us," Persimmon announced decisively, walking away from the quiet willow tree.

Chapter Eight

Hector circled the Sleepy Willow Tree silently. He wished he had a pair of binoculars. It would make it easier to see what those Raccoons were up to. Curly had used the Bird Network to track him down and Hector had been more than willing to spy on the Raccoons. They were bad news as far as Hector was concerned. Why couldn't they move to the Beaver Lake area of Stanley Park? Ever since they had moved in, the Lost Lagoon neighborhood had gone to the ducks. Well, those ducks were another story! Riff raff as far as he was concerned.

"Hector, come in, Hector" Persimmon's voice crackled over the headset Hector was wearing.

"This is Blackbird One, Papa Bear," Hector replied. Silence for a moment from the other end.

"Umm, okay. Anyways, any sign of the Raccoons? Ah, over," Persimmon's voice asked.

"Negative, Papa Bear. Targets Riff and Raff are not in sight. Repeat, Riff and Raff have flown the coop, caw! I mean, over!" Hector could really get used to this under cover secret spy stuff.

"Ah, okay." Pause. "So Oscar and Felix aren't home? Please clarify, over," Persimmon requested.

"Affirmative," Hector said.

"Roger that, over," Persimmon answered.

"Roger? Roger who? Roger who?" Hector asked, confused.

"Roger, like you know? I understand, over."

"Who's Roger?" Hector asked, truly puzzled now.

There was silence for a moment before Persimmon answered. "Never mind," and there was a pause. "Over and out, Blackbird One. Keep your eyes open and let me know if you see them. Operation Egg In a Basket is about to commence. Over."

"A-okay, Papa Bear. Blackbird One over and out," Hector replied. It was time to find a comfortable tree to perch in where he could keep an eye on things.

* * *

Persimmon, Penelope and Curly stood at the base of the Sleepy Willow Tree. Curly had a length of rope coiled over his shoulder. Tied to the end was a reed basket that the Beavers had woven so the egg could be placed safely inside as Curly lowered it to the ground once he had found it.

"Okay, Curly. There's no sign of Oscar or Felix. All you have to do is climb up the tree, find the egg and lower it down to us. Wait for me to replace it with this," Persimmon produced a baseball from his rucksack and presented it to Penelope and Curly. Then he continued. "All you have to do is hoist this up and place it where you found the egg and voila. Operation complete."

"Where did you get that from?" Curly asked, amazement clear in his voice.

"From Gilly."

"Where did Gilly get a baseball?" Penelope asked.

"I'll tell you later. Now, let's get going before those Raccoons show up." Curly was beginning to look doubtful again, so Persimmon placed a gentle paw on his shoulder and squeezed reassuringly. "Remember, nothing's impossible, right?"

"Right," Curly agreed, resolved once more to do his part. He turned and scrambled up the willow tree.

The Raccoons had left their patio doors open so Curly slipped cautiously inside.

"Oh, I hope Hector was right," Curly mumbled to himself. His little knees were beginning to shake with nerves.

The Raccoons' place was filled with clutter. They had everything from twigs and marbles, spoons and popsicle sticks, to hats and key chains. Curly searched high and he searched low. All the while the sound of the clock that the Raccoons had

managed to collect kept ticking loudly in his ears. He was just
about to give up when he saw it. Nestled safely in a baseball
cap surrounded by a red scarf sat the pale bluish green egg.

Curly ran over to the egg and patted it gently. "It will be okay
now, little egg. We're going to take you home." Without any
hesitation, Curly carefully rolled the egg out of the baseball cap
nest and into the reed basket. Then he dragged the basket with
its precious cargo gingerly out the door. He went to the edge of
the tree and looked down.

"Psst! Persimmon! I found it! It's safe, too!" Curly called down
to his companions exuberantly.

"Lower it down carefully, Curly!" Persimmon urged.

"Okay!" Curly called back. He threw the other end of the rope
over a sturdy branch and began to painstakingly lower the frag-
ile egg down over the side of the Sleepy Willow Tree. *Please
don't let the raccoons show up now*! Curly wished fervently.

Curly didn't know how long it took to lower that egg down to
Persimmon and Penelope. It felt like it took all year, but finally,
just when Curly thought his arms couldn't take anymore, Persimmon grabbed the basket. He cradled the egg and basket in
his arms for a moment before passing it to Penelope.

"Take my Blackberry," he instructed Penelope as he helped her
to put the egg into the rucksack. "If for some reason you get
stopped by the Raccoons, call Ben. His number's on speed dial.

He's with the swans. They'll come to help you. Go."

Penelope turned to leave with her precious burden. She hesitated, turning back to Persimmon. "Do you think the baby will be okay? Do you think the egg will hatch?"

Persimmon thought for a moment. He really didn't know.

"With a little luck, Penelope. With a little luck," Persimmon said solemnly, trying to reassure them both. He smiled softly.

"Nothing's impossible," Penelope repeated. With a smile of her own, Penelope left to take the egg home.

Quickly, knowing that Curly was probably fretting terribly by now, Persimmon placed the baseball in the reed basket.

"Alright, Curly, it's good to go!" Persimmon called up in a loud whisper to the squirrel. Everything was going as planned.

Slowly the baseball began to rise up into the air. Too slowly.

"Curly! Is the other end of that rope long enough to throw down to me?"

The baseball in the basket stopped moving. After a moment, Curly's head appeared at the top of the willow tree.

"I think so. Just a few more pulls on my part." Curly sounded exhausted. The muscles in his little arms must be burning.

"You can do it, Curly," Persimmon said under his breath. The baseball fell a few centimeters before stopping altogether. "You can do it, Curly!" Persimmon encouraged his friend.

"Nothing…is…impossible!" Curly's determined voice travelled down to Persimmon. The baseball zoomed farther up the tree and seconds later the other end of the rope dangled down in front of Persimmon's face.

"That a boy, Curly!" Persimmon praised quietly. He couldn't wait to tell Curly how awesome he was. Persimmon grabbed the rope and pulled with all his might. One, two, three pulls and the baseball went up over the edge and disappeared from sight. Curly's head appeared over the side, a huge smile on his face. He waved at Persimmon before disappearing again.

Persimmon turned and leaned against the tree. They had done it! Operation Egg In a Basket was a success! He was just about to breathe a sigh of relief when he looked down the lane. There in the distance where two grayish brown balls of fur running, tumbling and wrestling down the lane towards the Sleepy Willow Tree.

"Hurry! Riff and Raff are in sight!" Persimmon whispered harshly, shaking the rope feverishly.

"Mission Impossible completed!" Curly crowed merrily and scampered down the tree. He had thrown the basket over the branch he had used to support the rope and it came tumbling down to land at Persimmon's feet. Before Curly reached the ground, Persimmon had begun to coil the rope in loops over his shoulder. Curly joined him and started to gather up the other end.

They couldn't go back over the stone bridge. The Raccoons would see them for sure. They would have to take the long way around the lagoon. Once out of earshot, Persimmon would contact Hector over the radio and get him to contact the swans. Matilda and Sorcha were searching the southern regions of the lake for possible treasures to bring to the Raccoons. They could meet up with him and Curly and sail them across the lake on their backs. The Raccoons would be none the wiser.

"Let's go! Follow me!" Persimmon said urgently. Squirrel and hare ran around the Sleepy Willow Tree and into the grasses, out of sight of the two approaching raccoons.

Just then it started to rain.

Chapter Nine

Persimmon sat upon Sorcha's back and Curly sat upon Matilda's. They had been met at the southern most point of Lost Lagoon's shore. They were gliding quickly over the rippling water, sheltered from the softly falling rain by the wings of the swans. Before long, they joined the group that was gathered silently around the nest of Queen Zoe and King Arthur.

Persimmon hopped down from Sorcha's back onto the log. Riding on a swan was nothing like surfing. It was exhilarating, but it was also serene and magical.

"Thank you, Sorcha."

"Thank you, young Persimmon," Sorcha replied, inclining her head. Persimmon nodded in return.

The group was silent and solemn. Queen Zoe and King Arthur stood over the egg on the nest opposite each other. Their foreheads were touching and the shape of the heads resting together like that formed a heart over their egg. Persimmon smiled. No matter what happened, the egg was surrounded by love.

Penelope took Persimmon's paw in hers and smiled. Persimmon squeezed her paw in return. Curly joined them on the log, making it bob up and down in the water just a little. Persimmon smiled down at him. Curly smiled and turned to focus his gaze on the egg.

Everyone who had helped today was present. Hector and Ben were there standing on the bank, and Persimmon noticed that Ben had managed to find his glasses. All the ducks were waddling around, quacking in low voices. The swans, Jasper and Sorcha, and William and Matilda were waiting silently and regally. Even Gilly had ventured out from his cozy little home to join them.

"I'd like to thank all of you. Without your help, our egg would never have been returned to us so quickly. You have our eternal gratitude," Queen Zoe stated earnestly. Her voice was thick with emotion she couldn't find words to express.

"Persimmon," King Arthur's deep voice addressed him, "if not for your courage, we would not have our egg. You have my deepest and most sincere thanks. You are truly a brave hare."

"You're most welcome, your Majesty," Persimmon responded politely. "But I didn't do this alone. Hector, Ben, and Penelope helped, too. Even Gilly helped out. It was a team effort. But if it hadn't been for Curly, none of this would have been possible. He showed the most selfless courage and faced his fears to bring your egg home to you. He is the real hero."

"Well then," said King Arthur. He turned to regard the little black squirrel with a regal and serious expression. Curly quivered nervously to be under such scrutiny. "Kneel, Curly Squirrelly," the King commanded imperiously.

Curly knelt on wobbly knees. "Y-yes, your Majesty?"

"In honor of your bravery and courage and unwavering care for others before yourself, I dub you Sir Curly Squirrelly of Stanley Park." King Arthur tapped his beak firmly on first one of Curly's shoulders and then the other. "Rise, Sir Knight of Stanley Park."

Sir Curly Squirrelly rose in delight. His eyes were wide with wonder and his beaming smile was filled with joy. His little chest puffed out with pride. He was a knight!

Everyone cheered loudly, clapping and flapping, honking and quacking and cawing with cheer.

"As for your part in the rescue," King Arthur said after the cheers died down, "Persimmon, Penelope, Ben, Hector, Gilly, as well as your canine friend Mercutio wherever he is, I make you guardians of Lost Lagoon." There was more cheering and back slapping and happy smiles all around.

"As soon as our egg hatches, we will have a festival to celebrate how our friends came together to help us. We will celebrate the kindness and generosity of our friends," Queen Zoe announced. Everybody cheered again. It would be rude not to. But nobody knew for certain if the egg would hatch. All they could do was hope and watch and wait.

Persimmon looked at all his friends, happy that everyone was together again. He looked mournfully at the egg. He hoped it would hatch. It would be a miracle.

Suddenly it stopped raining and everyone looked up at the sky. The clouds were parting and a beautiful rainbow was emerging. Persimmon looked down at the egg, resting quietly and still in the nest. Just then a bright ray of warm and gentle, golden sunlight shone down upon the egg. And then the egg quivered and moved a tiny little bit. It was as if the tiny little cygnet inside was welcoming the sunshine, eager to hatch into the world.

Yet, it lasted just a moment, and then it was still again. And Persimmon wondered if he had just imagined it all. But he was filled with hope.

After all, anything was possible.

* * *

Back at the Sleepy Willow Tree, the brothers Oscar and Felix Raccoon lay on their bellies watching the baseball they believed to be an egg. When Curly had swapped the egg with the baseball, he had wrapped it up tight in the red scarf so only a small part of the surface was showing. He had tucked it back into the baseball cap, and as yet, the Raccoons were none the wiser.

Felix was resting his chin on his front paws. "Why isn't it hatching?" he asked, confounded.

"Maybe you have to sit on it," Oscar answered, drumming his fingers on the floor of their messy and cluttered house.

So they waited, and they waited, and they waited some more, but that is another story.

Tale of the Lost Swan Egg

About the Author Kyra Dawson

Kyra Dawson has dreamed of being a writer and author since she was eight years old. There hasn't been a time in her life when she doesn't remember not having that dream. She has always wanted to create stories that would entertain, move you to laugh, and even touch your heart.

She makes her home in Vancouver, in beautiful British Columbia, Canada. In fact, Persimmon, his friends, and their world were inspired by one of her many excursions through Stanley Park and the up close and personal interactions with the animal inhabitants of the park.

Kyra has a knack for creating names and taglines, and is also a blogger, editor, freelance writer, and now an author. She reviews books and movies and is a regular contributor for TheMoviePool.com.

In her spare time you can find Kyra watching movies, reading, enjoying nature, or spinning tales. She is a mother of one precocious Youngling, a fuzzy cat who thinks he's a person, and a feisty fish who likes kissing. A lover of fairy tales, myths, and magic, Kyra has always believed that dreams really do come true.

Visit Kyra at www.BrighterScribe.com or www.TheScribesDesk.com. You can follow her on Twitter @BrighterScribe or @TheScribesDesk, and you can be her friend via Brighter Scribe on Facebook.

The Persimmon Tales - Book 1
Adventures in Stanley Park

For a complete glossary of terms and places used in this novel, as well as full character persona, please see the associated website: www.PersimmonTales.com.

Watch for Book 2 in the Persimmon Tales series - coming out soon.

See also the companion series The Chimona Chronicles by Rosie Reay. In a similar style, these stories are of critters that come alive and interact with humans on the Okanagan Lake shore.

Kyra is the editor of this series. See www.chimona.com. They are also illustrated by Candice McMullan.

Published by:

Foden Press ™

Children's Books
Business and How To Do It Books

www.FodenPress.com

LaVergne, TN USA
22 January 2011
213506LV00004B/34/P